Bobby Brewster's Ghost

Through his appearances on television and radio, and the story-telling sessions he has held in libraries, schools and at parties in Australia, New Zealand and South Africa as well as in almost every part of Britain, H. E. Todd can claim to be the best-known story-teller in the world.

Here are eight stories about his favourite character, Bobby Brewster, the boy to whom the most extraordinary things happen.

Bobby Brewster's Ghost

H. E. Todd

Illustrated by Lilian Buchanan

KNIGHT BOOKS
Hodder and Stoughton

Text copyright © 1966 H. E. Todd
Illustrations copyright © 1966 Hodder and Stoughton Ltd

First published in 1966 as *Bobby Brewster and the Ghost*

This edition first published 1973
Seventh impression 1984

Set, printed and bound in Great Britain for
Hodder and Stoughton Paperbacks, a
division of Hodder and Stoughton Ltd,
Mill Road, Dunton Green, Sevenoaks, Kent
(Editorial Office: 47 Bedford Square,
London, WC1 3DP) by
Cox & Wyman Ltd, Reading

ISBN 0 340 17222 3

Contents

The fat and jolly ghost   *page* 9

Tail twitch   19

The indiarubber   30

The paintbox   40

Mickey the monkey puppet   50

Roundabout horse   59

Unfair to sardines   71

Six pints, please!   83

Introduction

As you may know, funny things are always happening to Bobby Brewster, and now he's even met a funny ghost! At least, I thought his ghost adventure was funny, and that's why I wrote a story about it when he told me. I hope you think some of his other adventures in this book are funny, too. As long as he goes on having his adventures, you may be sure that I shall go on writing about them, so I hope you enjoy it.

After telling my stories in libraries and schools I have received many interesting letters from boys and girls suggesting titles for more stories. Some of the stories in this book have been written as a result of these suggestions, and I am very grateful to Josephine Dungey, Angela Field, Janet Hawke, Pamela Hewitt, Sylvia Kay, Rochelle Rose, Diane Rutherford, Colin Blake, David Marsden and Richard Torrance.

H. E. TODD

The fat and jolly ghost

It was a cold, clear afternoon last January and Bobby Brewster was staying with his Aunt Beatrice and Uncle Benjamin in their pretty Midlands village. All the morning he had played and read indoors, and sometimes looked out of the window to admire the white frost on the gaunt trees in the garden. Then, in the early afternoon, a pale sun peeped through the clouds and Bobby felt he could stay inside no longer.

'Can I please go for a little walk, Aunt Beatrice?' he asked. 'It looks so lovely outside.'

'Yes,' said his aunt, 'but don't stay out for long. Remember it's midwinter, and when the sun disappears it will be very dull and cold. So wrap yourself up well, keep moving, and don't go far.'

Bobby put on his wellington boots, his muffler, and his overcoat, and trotted along the road. He climbed over the stile by the vicarage wall and into the field which everyone calls 'Baldwin's Field'. There was something peculiar about it.

'I know what it is,' said Bobby Brewster to himself. 'I've never noticed the wood at the bottom of this field before. I must go and walk in it.'

So he did.

Everything was very still, except for the crunch of Bobby's footsteps on the fallen leaves. He looked on the ground and noticed each separate blade of grass standing stiffly to attention. Then he raised his eyes and saw silver whiskers of frost on the branches of the trees against the pale blue sky. It was beautiful but mysterious.

At that moment a fat and jolly-looking man stepped out on to the path from behind a tree. He was wearing the most extraordinary old fashioned clothes, just like some of the pictures in history books.

'Hullo, young man,' he said to Bobby Brewster.

'Good afternoon, sir,' replied Bobby, with his eyes nearly popping out of his head.

'You seem surprised to see me,' said the fat and jolly man.

'I am rather,' agreed Bobby. 'Are you going to a fancy-dress party?'

'Certainly not,' said the man. 'Why do you ask?'

'It's your clothes,' said Bobby Brewster. 'They're funny.'

'They seem perfectly all right to me,' said the man. 'Anyway, what are *you* doing here?'

'Just going for a walk,' said Bobby. 'I've never been in this wood before.'

'I don't suppose you have,' said the fat and jolly man. 'Do you like it?'

'It's very beautiful,' said Bobby. 'But it's rather spooky.'

'Spooky? What do you mean?' asked the man.

'Full of ghosts,' replied Bobby.

'That's nothing to worry about,' said the man.

'It is for me,' said Bobby. 'I'm frightened of ghosts.'

'Why?' asked the man. 'Have you ever seen one?'

'No,' said Bobby. 'Have you?'

'Lots of them,' replied the man. 'They're quite harmless.'

'I'm glad you think so,' said Bobby.

'I not only think so, I'm sure of it,' said the man. 'And I ought to know.'

'Why?' asked Bobby.

'Because I'm a ghost myself,' said the man.

'Don't be silly,' said Bobby Brewster. 'You're far too fat and jolly for a ghost.'

'Very well, I'll prove it,' said the man – and he disappeared.

'Hi!' called Bobby. 'Where *are* you?'

'I'm still here, but you can't see me,' said a voice. '*Now* do you believe I'm a ghost?'

'Yes,' cried Bobby.

'And you still aren't afraid of me?' asked the voice.

'No,' cried Bobby Brewster.

'Very well, I'll come back,' said the voice. And the fat and jolly man appeared again, looking fatter and jollier than ever. 'There you are, that proves it,' he said. 'My name is Sir William Baldwin. I was fat and jolly when I was alive two hundred years ago, so I jolly well don't see why I shouldn't be a fat and jolly ghost. I suppose you expected me to be dressed all in white and making silly ghostly noises, didn't you?'

'Yes, Sir William, as a matter of fact I did,' agreed Bobby Brewster.

'I guessed as much,' said Sir William. 'You ought to see my great-grandfather, Sir Marmaduke Baldwin. He acts silly like that. He never did anybody any good when he was alive, and now he thinks the only way he can have any effect is by going all ghostly. Would you like to meet him?'

'Er – very well,' said Bobby, but he sounded rather doubtful.

'There's no need for alarm,' said Sir William. 'Just take no notice. He's quite harmless really.' And he went to the edge of the path and shouted 'MALMY!'

'Hullo,' replied a deep voice – and it did sound rather ghostly.

'Come here and show yourself,' shouted Sir William.

A figure dressed in white from head to foot slid silently out from the wood. As soon as it saw Bobby Brewster it raised its arms and said in a deep voice – 'B-o-o-o-o-o-h'.

Bobby tried to cling to Sir William's arm, but he couldn't because there wasn't anything to cling to, although Sir William could be seen quite clearly. When the ghostly figure saw Bobby looking frightened, it raised its white arms higher still and said, louder and lower – 'B-O-O-O-O-O-H'.

Bobby Brewster jumped.

'Don't talk nonsense, Malmy,' said Sir William sharply. 'Booo indeed. It doesn't mean anything anyway. And why are you all in white? You know Lady Baldwin objects to silly play-acting. She was complaining only yesterday about the crumpled state of some of the sheets. If you don't behave yourself, I will tell her you've been playing ghosts again.'

Sir Marmaduke lowered his arms at once.

'*Please* don't do that,' he pleaded. 'I promised her I wouldn't, and you know what she's like when she's annoyed.'

'Very well,' said the fat and jolly Sir William. 'I won't tell her this time on one condition. Take your sheet off and do that other silly ghost act that you're always trying to frighten people with.'

'Must I?' asked Sir Marmaduke, looking foolish.

'Yes, you must,' said Sir William. 'I want to show this young friend of mine just how stupid ghosts can get.'

Sir Marmaduke took off his sheet and folded it carefully, so that Lady Marmaduke would never know he had been wearing it. Then he took some long chains out of his pocket, fixed them round his ankles, and shuffled about in them clanking.

'Go on,' said Sir William. 'That's not all. Do the rest of the act.'

'No, PLEASE,' pleaded Sir Marmaduke.

'If you don't, I'll tell Lady Baldwin about the sheet,' threatened Sir William.

Sir Marmaduke quickly took his head off his shoulders and tucked it underneath his left arm.

'Now say your little piece,' demanded Sir William.

Sir Marmaduke clanked about in his chains saying in a deep voice 'I am the ghost of Sir Marmaduke Baldwin.' But the expression on his face wasn't at all ferocious to match the words. He

looked so sheepish that Bobby Brewster started to giggle.

'There you are, I told you it was silly to be frightened of ghosts,' said Sir William. 'And the more horrid they look, the more helpless they are. Take *him*, for instance. He's just a sham. He wasn't even beheaded. As a matter of fact, he died through eating too much apple-pie – didn't you, Malmy?'

'Yes,' said Sir Marmaduke, and saying it under his arm looked more absurd than ever.

'Very well, you can go now,' said Sir William to Sir Marmaduke. 'Don't forget to take your sheet with you.'

Sir Marmaduke slunk away, looking ashamed of himself. By this time the pale sun had gone behind the clouds and the wood was beginning to look darker.

'I say,' said Bobby Brewster, 'I'm very sorry but I *must* get home, or Aunt Beatrice will be worrying. Thank you very much for being so kind and proving that there's no need to be frightened of ghosts any more.'

'That's all right,' said Sir William kindly.

'Not that I would ever be frightened of you,' added Bobby. 'You're far too fat and jolly.'

'Yes, and I intend to remain that way,' said Sir William. 'Goodbye, young man.'

'Goodbye, Sir William,' said Bobby Brewster. 'Can I see you again sometime?'

'Maybe,' said Sir William. 'But I'm making no promises' – and he disappeared.

Bobby trotted back through the field. As he was climbing over the stile he met the vicar.

'Hullo, Bobby,' said the vicar. 'Where have you been?'

'I've been for a walk in Baldwin's Wood, sir,' said Bobby.

'Baldwin's what?' asked the vicar in a surprised voice.

'Baldwin's Wood, sir,' said Bobby. 'The wood at the bottom of Baldwin's Field,' and he turned round to point it out.

But it wasn't there any more. Baldwin's Wood had disappeared.

Tail twitch

One of the silliest things you can do is to leave bottles lying about on the beach at the seaside. Leaving bottles lying about *anywhere* is bad enough, because litter spoils the country-side, but on the beach it is dangerous as well. The glass breaks on the rocks and people tread on it and injure themselves. A boy I know once had his holiday completely ruined through cutting his foot during his first day at the seaside.

Of course there are times when empty bottles come in useful at sea. I heard the other day of a man who was shipwrecked and floating on a raft with nothing but a crate of Coca-Cola and a case full of sardines. He threw an empty Coca-Cola bottle overboard with a message in it asking for help. Luckily the bottle floated to the shore and someone found the message, but that was several days later. By the time the poor man was rescued he was nearly floating in the air through drinking so much Coca-Cola, and from that day to this he has never eaten another sardine, not even in a sandwich. However, that has nothing to do with this story, which is about a funny thing that happened to Bobby Brewster when he was staying at the seaside last summer.

One morning while he was paddling, Bobby noticed a bottle bobbing about in the sea. Like a sensible boy he waded out to fetch it, so that it wouldn't get broken. Imagine his surprise when he found a piece of paper tucked inside, with a message on it. This is what it said in funny, squiggly writing:

> *I need help. Please come to the cave in Smugglers' Bay. It's a secret, so don't tell anyone.*
>
> *Minnie*

Wasn't that exciting? Bobby knew the cave in Smugglers' Bay, because he had explored it earlier in the week. It wasn't very far away and there was nothing dangerous there. He had never heard of Minnie, but from the note she sounded very polite. So that afternoon, when his mother and father were snoozing in the sun – as mothers and fathers often do on the beach – he scrambled over the rocks to Smugglers' Bay. There was no one to be seen on the beach, and when he reached the cave he looked inside. It was dark, with a deep pool of water which the tide had left behind, but there was no sign of Minnie anywhere.

'Hullo,' shouted Bobby into the cave.

'Ullo–ullo–ullo–ullo,' came back his echo, but no one answered him. He tried again.

'Minnie,' he shouted.

'Innie–innie–innie–innie,' went the echo.

Then a very funny thing happened. Lots of bubbles plopped to the top of the pool, and a girl's face with long, scraggy hair popped up.

'I'm so glad you've come,' said the girl. Then she cried a short, sharp 'OOH,' and nearly shot out of the water.

Bobby thought that was rather peculiar, but he was too polite to say anything. 'Who are you?' he asked.

'I'm Minnie,' said the girl. 'OOH,' and she shot out of the water again.

'I found your note in the bottle,' said Bobby

Brewster, 'and came to see if I could help.'

'That's very kind of you,' said Minnie. 'OOH' – and shot up again.

'I say, is something wrong?' asked Bobby.

'Yes,' said Minnie. 'OOH, that's why I sent the message, OOH.'

'It sounds very painful,' said Bobby in alarm.

'It's not so much painful as inconvenient,' said Minnie. 'OOH.'

'What is it?' asked Bobby.

'I've got a twitching tail,' said the girl. 'OOH.'

'Tail, did you say?' asked Bobby in surprise.

'Yes, tail,' repeated Minnie. 'I'm a mermaid, you see.' Then she twitched over to the side of the pool and sat on a rock, still twitching.

Bobby had never seen a mermaid before, but he tried not to stare too hard. There was no doubt that she found her twitching tail most trying.

'Oh dear,' said Bobby Brewster. 'What can we do about your poor tail?'

'I haven't the slightest idea,' said Minnie the mermaid. 'The trouble is that no other mermaid has ever suffered from tail twitch before, so we don't know what to do. OOH– I can't even swim out to sea, because when my tail twitches– OOH – I jerk round and round in circles– OOH–'

'Had I better fetch a doctor?' suggested Bobby.

'Oh no, you mustn't do that,' cried Minnie. 'Lots of people will get to hear about it and come and stare at me. OOH. Mermaids simply hate being stared at – OOH – That's why I asked you on my note not to tell anyone.'

Well, it was a real problem, wasn't it? They went on talking about it, and in between the OOHs Minnie told Bobby that inquiries about twitching tails had been made from all sorts of animals, but none of them could help. Dogs said they wagged their tails when they were pleased. Cats said they swished the ends of theirs when they were angry. As for cows and horses, they said they only waved their tails to keep the flies away. None of them had ever heard of tail twitch. So that wasn't much use, was it?

'What does it actually feel like?' asked Bobby Brewster.

'Like a very bad attack of hiccups,' said Minnie the mermaid – 'OOH.' Bobby didn't find that very surprising. After all, if you had a tail, you would probably twitch it when you had a bad attack of hiccups, wouldn't you?

'I know what I'll do,' said Bobby. 'I'll see what I can find out about curing hiccups, and come back tomorrow and tell you.'

'That's a jolly good idea,' said Minnie. 'Thank you very much for being so helpful. But don't tell anyone about me, will you?'

'Of course not,' said Bobby Brewster.

Then he ran back to his parents who were still snoozing in the sun. When they woke up they asked him if he had enjoyed his walk and he said

'Yes,' but he was most careful not to mention anything about mermaids.

Later that afternoon, when sitting in the lounge of the hotel, Bobby Brewster suddenly had a severe attack of hiccups. Between you and me he was only pretending. But don't tell anyone, will you, because he only wanted to find out what people would suggest to make him stop. He had to drink lots and lots of glasses of water, and one

silly man gave him a sharp slap on the back and then explained that the sudden shock might stop the hiccups. Bobby didn't stop hiccuping, though, because he thought that the silly man's ideas would probably be silly anyway, and he wanted to hear from someone sensible. Unfortunately that only encouraged the silly man, and he said he would have to try holding up Bobby by his feet with his head hanging down to see if that would work. He jolly nearly did try it too, but luckily Dr Wilkinson – who was a guest at the hotel – came in and saw what was happening. When he heard Bobby hiccuping, he said he would prepare a dose of medicine to cure it.

The dose tasted perfectly horrid, and Bobby almost wished he hadn't pretended to have hiccups. They stopped suddenly after one small spoonful of medicine. And then Bobby asked Dr Wilkinson if he could keep the rest of the dose in the bottle in case his hiccups came back. Dr Wilkinson said, 'Yes, as long as you promise only to take one small spoonful at a time,' and Bobby said there was no fear of his ever wanting to have more than that.

The next morning Bobby hid the bottle of hiccup medicine in his pocket, and at the first opportunity he ran round to the cave in Smugglers' Bay.

'Minnie-innie-innie-innie,' he called, and she popped up from the pool, twitching like anything.

'I'm so glad you've come,' she said. 'I've been having the most frightful tail twitch. Have you found anything?'

'I've brought you a dose of hiccup mixture,' said Bobby Brewster. 'I don't think you'll like it much, but a real doctor gave it to me, so I think it might work.'

Then he handed her the bottle. 'Oh dear,' he said, 'I forgot to bring a spoon.'

'Never mind,' said Minnine, and before he could stop her she had pulled out the cork and poured a mouthful of the stuff into her mouth.

'FAUGH,' she cried, and jumped about in the pool, twitching so hard that the water looked as if it was boiling. Bobby became quite alarmed until suddenly she stopped.

'What horrid stuff,' cried Minnie, making a face.

'Well, I did warn you,' said Bobby – 'and, anyway, it worked.'

It had too. Without realizing it, Minnie had completely stopped twitching her tail. She could hardly believe it was true, but it was. She even *tried* to twitch her tail, and could only manage a feeble wobble.

'What a relief,' she said. 'It was even worth taking that frightful medicine. Thank you very much indeed for all your trouble. Now I can swim properly again. Look at me.'

She dived deep into the pool and swam smoothly around.

'I wish I could swim like that,' said Bobby Brewster enviously.

'So you shall,' said Minnie the mermaid. 'It's the least I can do to teach you how to swim like me after the help you've been. Come round here to the cave every morning in your bathing trunks for the rest of your holiday, and I will give you swimming lessons.'

So that was what Bobby Brewster did, and by the time the week was over he had learned to swim just like Minnie the mermaid.

When Bobby dived into the waves on the last day of his holiday to show his mother and father how well he could swim, they were absolutely amazed. Then Mr Brewster said a very funny thing.

'I've never seen anyone learn so quickly,' he said proudly to Mrs Brewster. 'Bobby seems to have taken to the sea just like a mermaid!'

Which was an even truer remark than he knew, wasn't it?

The indiarubber

It looked like an ordinary indiarubber, and Bobby Brewster bought it from an ordinary man in an ordinary shop. If the ordinary man in the ordinary shop had guessed that it was a magic indiarubber, I doubt if he would have sold it for five pence. But he didn't guess. Nor would you or I have guessed if we had bought it from him. Even Bobby Brewster himself knew nothing about it until later, when some very funny things started happening.

The first funny thing happened on the day after Bobby's birthday, when Bobby sat down to write a 'thank you' letter. This is what he wrote to Aunt Beatrice and Uncle Benjamin:

> *Dere Arnt and Unkle,*
>> *Thank you verry much for the choklits.*
> *They are luvly.*
>> *Luv from*
>>> *Bobby*

Then as he went to the desk to fetch an envelope his mother said to him, 'Bobby, I'm pleased to see that you are writing a "thank you" letter without being asked. May I read it?'

'Certainly,' said Bobby, and handed it to her. Mrs Brewster looked puzzled.

'What ever does it mean?' she asked.

'What it says, of course,' said Bobby. He didn't mean to be rude, although he sounded it.

'But it doesn't mean anything,' said Mrs Brewster.

'It's quite clear to me, anyway,' said Bobby.

'Are you sure?' said his mother. 'I think you had better read it again.'

So he did and this is what he saw:

    and   ,
   Thank you   *much for the*
 They are   .
    from
    Bobby

'This isn't what I wrote,' cried Bobby Brewster.
'Half of it has been rubbed out.'

'Well, you're the one with the rubber,' said
Mrs Brewster.

'But it's a new rubber and I've never used it,'
said Bobby. 'Look at it.'

They both looked carefully at the new india-rubber.

'If you haven't used it, somebody else has,' said Mrs Brewster. 'There's a corner rubbed off and, besides, there are some specks of rubber on the letter in the spaces.'

'So there are,' agreed Bobby. 'I don't understand it at all.'

'You must have been dreaming when you used it,' said his mother, and Bobby thought that perhaps he had. Anyway, he filled in the blanks, and, between you and me, he was a little more careful over his spelling this time.

The following morning Bobby was in Mr Limcano's class at school, and they had sums. Bobby neatly laid out his pencils and new indiarubber on his desk in readiness.

'Now, boys,' said Mr Limcano. 'We'll do some mental arithmetic for a change. I'm going to ask you three questions, and you must write the answers down on a piece of paper. Then when we have finished you can pass your papers to the next boy for checking. Here is the first question. What is seven plus eight?'

Bobby Brewster wrote down thirteen without thinking and felt very proud of himself for being so quick about it.

'If four men built a house in four months, how long would eight men take to build a house?' asked Mr Limcano.

'That's easy,' said Bobby to himself. 'Eight, of course.' And he wrote it down.

'A man went into a shop and bought four apples for two pence each. How much change would he get from ten pence?' asked Mr Limcano.

This time Bobby had to think because there were two things to work out. So he took a little more time and then wrote down two pence.

'Now hand on your papers, boys,' said Mr Limcano, and Bobby passed his to Billy Singleton, who was sitting at the next desk.

'The answer to the first question is fifteen,' said Mr Limcano. 'Has anybody got it wrong?'

'Please, sir,' said Billy Singleton, 'Bobby Brewster hasn't answered it at all.'

'I have,' cried Bobby Brewster.

'Well, there's nothing on your paper, anyway,' said Billy Singleton.

'Never mind about that now,' said Mr Limcano. 'I'm afraid I can't give you a mark, Bobby. Now the answer to the second question, which had a catch in it. If four men could build a house in four months, eight men could build it in two months, and not eight months, which I'm sure lots of boys have written down.'

'Please, sir,' said Billy Singleton, 'I'm not trying to tell stories, but Bobby Brewster didn't answer that question either.'

'I did,' cried Bobby indignantly. 'I got it wrong, but I wrote down eight months.'

'There's nothing on your paper,' said Billy. 'You only wrote down the answer to the third question.'

'And what was his answer?' asked Mr Limcano.

'Two pence, sir,' said Billy Singleton.

'He happens to be right for once,' said Mr Limcano. 'At least you get one mark, Bobby.'

'But, sir, I answered the other questions as well, honestly I did, even if I did get them wrong,' protested Bobby Brewster.

'Show me his paper, Billy,' said Mr Limcano

and Billy Singleton took Bobby's paper up to the front of the class.

Mr Limcano looked at it. 'You rubbed out the other two answers before handing this over,' he said.

'I didn't, sir,' cried Bobby.

'Then you rubbed them out, Billy, after the paper was handed to you,' said Mr Limcano.

'No, sir, not me, sir,' said Billy Singleton.

'Well, there are distinct signs of rubbing out,' said Mr Limcano. 'Bobby, you had better come and see me after the class is finished.'

At the end of the morning Mr Limcano asked Bobby to show him his rubber.

'There you are,' said Mr Limcano, pointing to the newly rubbed corner. 'Someone has been using it recently.'

'I know it sounds silly, sir,' said Bobby, 'but I think there is something funny about my india-rubber.' And he told Mr Limcano about the 'thank you' letter he had written the day before.

'Bless my soul,' said Mr Limcano. 'There is indeed something peculiar about it. This needs investigation. Would you be kind enough to lend

your indiarubber to me? I want to try some experiments.'

'Certainly, sir,' said Bobby. And he did.

The next morning when Bobby arrived at school, Mr Limcano called him aside.

'That indiarubber of yours is most extraordinary,' he said. 'It rubs things out all by itself. First of all I was in the middle of a difficult crossword puzzle and had to answer the front door. When I got back several letters had been rubbed out. And do you know, they all turned out to be the letters I had put down wrongly.'

'Goodness gracious me,' said Bobby Brewster.

'But that's not all,' continued Mr Limcano. 'Later in the evening I tried to work out a very complicated sum, and I couldn't for the life of me get it right. Then the telephone rang, and when I had finished talking, I returned to my sum and found that some of the figures had been rubbed out. They were figures that had been wrong, and so I was able to fill them in correctly and finish the sum quite easily.'

'That's jolly useful, sir,' said Bobby. 'We've got our exams tomorrow, so may I have my rubber back, please?'

'No, you certainly may not,' said Mr Limcano. 'The very idea. I don't like rubbing out on examination papers, anyway. And I'm certainly not going to allow you to use an indiarubber that rubs out all your mistakes for you. I'll give it back to you at the end of the term after the exams are over.'

'What a pity, sir,' said Bobby – but secretly he didn't blame Mr Limcano.

Well, the story hasn't quite finished even to this day, because Bobby Brewster still has a tiny piece of his magic indiarubber left. It has proved very useful to him since he first found out that it was magic, too.

You see, he is so anxious for it to last as long as possible and not to rub itself right away, that he takes much more care than he used to when he is writing his answers. So nowadays there is far less need for anything to be rubbed out, and the magic indiarubber looks like lasting much longer than at first seemed likely. Bobby always keeps it handy, though, just in case. Except at exams, that is, when Mr Limcano sees to it that the rubber is hidden away.

There's something else that perhaps I ought to mention before finishing the story. Bobby Brewster has found that it is not the slightest use writing down mistakes on purpose and hoping to see the magic rubber hop over by itself and rub them out. For one thing, it refuses to take any notice when people are trying to be too clever, and for another, it refuses to perform any magic when people are looking.

And I don't blame it, do you?

The paintbox

It wasn't his birthday. It wasn't Christmas time. It wasn't even an exciting day of the week like Saturday. It was just an ordinary wet Tuesday afternoon when Uncle Benjamin called, quite unexpectedly, with a parcel under his arm which he handed to Bobby Brewster.

'Is this for me, Uncle?' asked Bobby, in surprise.

'Of course it is, Bobby,' said Uncle Benjamin. 'Otherwise I wouldn't have given it to you, would I?'

'Oh thank you, Uncle,' said Bobby. 'May I open it now please?'

'Certainly you may,' said Uncle Benjamin. 'If you want to know what it is.'

So he did – and what do you think it was? A new paintbox. It was, really. Complete with little square pots of paint of all colours in the rainbow and two paint-brushes.

'Oh thank you, Uncle,' cried Bobby again. 'It's just what I want.'

'Good,' said Uncle Benjamin. 'But don't make too much of a mess, will you?'

'I'll try not to,' said Bobby, and ran upstairs to his bedroom with it.

When he opened the paintbox again Bobby Brewster said to himself, 'It seems almost a shame to use it, doesn't it? It looks so clean and fresh and I know what'll happen. I'll spill water on it and the colours will run and probably splash on the carpet.'

Then he thought again. 'But what's the use of just looking at it? It's meant to be used. I'm jolly well going to have a try.' So he fetched some water and a large piece of white paper, and in no time at all the paper wasn't white at all, but a splash of brilliant colours.

After a time he became tired of splashing colours and decided to try and paint a picture of the Brewster garden. I'm afraid he wasn't very sensible about it though. Instead of taking the trouble to work out the proper colours, he used whatever came easily. The result was an extraordinary-looking picture of black sky, dark blue trees and a red lawn.

Then a very funny thing happened. Indeed, it was more than funny. It was quite extraordinary.

While Bobby had been painting his picture, he had not noticed that the grey sky outside had been turning darker and darker. Suddenly, through a break in the black clouds, an angry red sun threw rays of light on the lawn. For a few moments, before the clouds closed up again, the Brewsters' trees really did look dark blue, and the Brewsters' lawn really did look red.

'Goodness gracious me,' said Bobby to himself. 'My paints must have known what was going to happen. Certainly I could never have guessed. It was just a fluke and, anyway, no one would believe me if I said our garden ever did look like that.'

Which was perfectly true, because when Bobby showed his picture to his mother, she said, 'Yes dear, it's quite nice, but who ever heard of blue trees and red grass?'

Later that week Bobby was feeling rather silly. I expect you do sometimes, don't you? And you simply have to do something silly before you can be sensible again. Well, the silly thing that Bobby did was to get hold of an old photograph of his mother and father which he found lying about. He took it upstairs and worked on it with his paints. By the time he had finished, his father had long, curly, yellow hair and a red moustache, and his mother had a bright green nose.

That made Bobby feel better. I can't think why it should, but it did – so he slipped the ridiculous-looking photograph in his desk drawer and ran downstairs and behaved quite normally for the rest of the day.

The next day was Saturday, when the Brewsters often get up a little later than usual. When he woke that morning, Bobby was not only feeling sensible but helpful as well, and he decided to go downstairs to the kitchen and make his parents some early morning tea. He laid the tray and boiled the water carefully in the kettle. First he warmed the teapot as he had been taught, and then he put in one spoonful of tea for his mother, one for his father, and one for the pot. After filling it with water, he carried it upstairs on the tray. He laid it quietly on the bedside table and tapped his father on the shoulder.

'Why, thank you Bobby. How kind of you,' said Mr Brewster in a sleepy voice, and sat up. At once Bobby started laughing. In fact he laughed so loudly that he woke his mother and she started laughing too.

'What are you laughing at?' asked Mr Brewster.

'At you, of course,' said Mrs Brewster.

'Why at me, of course?' asked Mr Brewster.

'Just look in the mirror,' she replied. 'You've grown long, curly, yellow hair and a red moustache.'

You might think that this would have shocked Mr Brewster, but in fact he started laughing too.

'I'm surprised you think you're funny,' said Mrs Brewster.

'You're a fine one to talk,' said Mr Brewster. 'I'm not laughing at myself. I'm laughing at you. You look in the mirror too. You've got a bright green nose.'

'What!' cried Mrs Brewster, and by the time they had both rushed to look in the mirror, they didn't think it was funny any more. In fact they both felt distinctly worried. Mr Brewster said that he couldn't possibly go to the barber's to have his hair cut and moustache shaved off, because he would never be able to explain how they had grown like that overnight. Mrs Brewster said it was all very well for him, because the barber would at least be able to cut his hair and moustache off, but what about her? She didn't even know whom to see about a bright green nose, and anyone she did see would probably only laugh.

While they were still arguing about it, Bobby had an idea. He slipped away to his bedroom and took out the photograph of his mother and father. He carefully washed away the yellow hair, red moustache and green nose which he had painted on the day before. When he returned to his parents' bedroom his mother was busy scrubbing her nose at the hand-basin, and his father was sitting on the bed furiously combing his hair.

'There's no need to comb so hard,' said Bobby.

'I'm trying to get rid of these silly curls,' explained his father.

'You have got rid of them,' said Bobby. 'Your hair is just as it used to be.'

'What!' cried Mr Brewster, and ran to the mirror.

'Goodness gracious me, how did that happen?' he asked.

'How did what happen?' asked Mrs Brewster through the soap-suds.

'My hair has gone back to normal,' explained Mr Brewster. Then he looked more closely at his

wife. 'What's more,' he said, 'if you rub the soap off your nose, I think you'll find it's not green any more.'

So she did, and it wasn't. And you can be quite sure that they were very relieved not to have to go out and do their Saturday shopping with yellow curls, a red moustache and a bright green nose.

Well, naturally, after all the excitement had died down, Bobby went back to his bedroom to think. 'There's only one explanation,' he said to himself. 'These are magic paints and they only like painting things as they really are. So if I paint anything silly with them, the thing goes all silly just to prove that the paints are right. It happened when I painted the garden black, dark-blue and red, and it happened again when I gave Father yellow hair and a red moustache and Mother a green nose on their photograph. I shall have to be more careful in future.'

And he was. Much more careful. Indeed his painting improved so much that one of his pictures was in the place of honour at the exhibition next school prize day. It was called 'My garden, by Robert Brewster,' and in it the trees and lawn were actually green.

Since that day there *has* been one awkward moment. Bobby was in another one of his silly moods, and he started looking at a school photograph which he had brought home the day before. And the more he looked at it, the sillier he felt.

'Wouldn't it be simply marvellous,' he said to himself, 'if Mr Limcano came to school tomorrow morning with long black hair like King Charles the Second and found Billy Singleton and Willie

Watson sitting in front of the class with bright green noses?' Then a mischievous look came into his face, and he could resist the thought no longer. So he carried the photograph upstairs with itching fingers, put it on his desk, and fetched his new paintbox.

But, do you know, a very funny thing happened. However hard Bobby tried, he simply could not open the lid of that paintbox, although it had always opened perfectly easily before and has done since. In the end his fingers got so tired with pulling and pressing, that he had to give up the idea of painting silly things on his school photograph, and I'm sure you'll agree that it's just as well he did.

Which all goes to prove that his paintbox is not only magic, but sensible as well, doesn't it?

Mickey
the monkey puppet

Aunt Angela visited the Brewsters the other day, still wearing her wobbly ear-rings as usual. The first thing she said to Bobby was:

'Come and give your old Aunt Angela a great big kiss.'

Bobby did as he was asked, looking rather red in the face. Then Aunt Angela held him away from her, gazed at him, and said:

'Why, Bobby darling, how you've grown.'

Bobby said nothing. There was nothing much he could say, was there? After all, as Aunt Angela hadn't seen him for over a year, he could hardly have shrunk, could he?

Then the time came for handing over the usual present. Of course, it is very kind of Aunt Angela to give him presents, but Bobby always feels so silly while she is doing it because she makes such a fuss. She dives into her bag and looks coy, and always says exactly the same thing:

'I've got something nice especially for you.'

Aunt Angela's idea of something nice is often different from Bobby's. The trouble is that she always forgets that he is a year older than when she last saw him, and so she gives him something babyish. Sometimes she even forgets what she gave him before, and he has the same present more than once. He had baby rattles every year till he was four, which was rather silly. But, then I'm afraid Aunt Angela is rather silly herself, so perhaps that was hardly surprising.

As a matter of fact her last present was more sensible than usual, although Bobby didn't think so at first. It was a glove puppet with a monkey face, wearing a red hat with a gold tassel on top. Bobby wondered what to call it, until his mother said that it looked like an Irishman she knew, and then he christened it Mickey. Mickey the monkey puppet.

Have you ever used a glove puppet? It's quite easy because it actually fits like a glove. You slip your hand inside and put your middle finger in the neck of the puppet and your thumb and little finger in the arms. Then you waggle your fingers about and get very funny effects. After a few days Bobby became quite good at it and was able to make Mickey the monkey look as if he was really alive.

In fact he was actually alive in a funny sort of way. He was, really. And now I'll tell you how Bobby Brewster first found out.

At first, when he started playing with the monkey puppet, Bobby was able to control its arms quite easily, but after a time he found that his thumb always went straight round and touched the monkey's nose. He tried to stop it, but he couldn't. It kept on happening, until one evening Bobby said to himself, 'Keep still, you silly thing. What on earth are you trying to do?'

At least he thought he said it to himself, but he couldn't have done because a voice said:

'I'm only scratching my nose.'

'I beg your pardon?' asked Bobby Brewster.

'I said I'm only scratching my nose,' repeated the voice. 'It's itching.'

'I can't feel it,' said Bobby.

'Why should you?' said the voice. 'It's my nose that's itching, not yours.'

'Who are you?' asked Bobby.

'I'm Mickey the monkey puppet,' said the voice.

'Goodness gracious me,' said Bobby, 'I'm so sorry. I had no idea your nose was itching. Let me make it better.'

And he gave Mickey's nose a jolly good rubbing with his thumb.

'That's quite enough,' cried Mickey. 'There's no need to overdo it. And while we're talking, there's something I want you to promise.'

'Certainly, if it's reasonable,' said Bobby. 'What do you want?'

'Will you please stop fiddling about with your penknife so much?' said Mickey. 'Opening and closing the blade all the time makes me nervous.'

'Why?' asked Bobby.

'Because I'm afraid you might cut your middle finger,' said Mickey.

'There's no need for you to worry,' said Bobby. 'After all, it's my middle finger.'

'That's what you think,' said Mickey the monkey. 'It may be your middle finger most of the time, but when you put your glove puppet on I'd have you know it's my neck. And I don't like the idea of having my throat cut.'

'I don't blame you,' said Bobby. 'I'm sorry I hadn't thought of that. Of course I shall be more careful in future. Is there anything else I can do for you?'

'Well, yes, since you ask, there is,' said Mickey the monkey. 'I should like a nice feed.'

'What of?' asked Bobby. 'We have plenty of dog food and cat food in the house, but I'm afraid we don't keep monkey food.'

'Have you got any bananas?' asked Mickey.

'Lots of them,' answered Bobby. 'Mother bought a big bunch this morning.'

'They'll do,' said the monkey puppet.

Well, bananas may be very nice, but you can have too much of a good thing, can't you? Bobby had never seen anyone eat bananas like Mickey the monkey puppet. He peeled them one after the other and thrust them into his mouth, and they disappeared in no time. The funny thing was that, although Bobby was wearing the glove puppet, he didn't seem to have any control over it at all. He was horrified at the way the bananas were disappearing, but he could do nothing to stop it. In the end Mickey suddenly stopped eating and said:

'I feel sick.'

'I'm not surprised,' said Bobby. 'I don't feel very well myself.'

So he carefully put Mickey back in his toy cupboard and went up to bed.

The next morning Bobby still didn't feel well, and when his mother saw him at breakfast, she asked him what was the matter.

'I've got a pain in my hand,' said Bobby.

Mrs Brewster looked at it.

'I'm going to take you to the doctor's surgery this morning,' she said. 'Your middle finger is swollen, and there's a nasty lump on your hand.'

Doctor Hopkins's waiting-room was crowded as usual. Bobby and his mother had to sit for half an hour listening to people talking about their illnesses. Bobby thought to himself that the funny thing was that the more ill they thought they were, the prouder they seemed to be of themselves. Then at last his turn came, and into Doctor Hopkins's surgery he went with his mother.

'Will you please look at Bobby's hand, doctor?' said Mrs Brewster. 'He complains that it's painful and it looks very swollen.'

'It does indeed,' said Doctor Hopkins. Then he inspected the swollen hand more carefully.

'This is very curious,' he said. 'I've never seen anything quite like it.'

Doctor Hopkins did practically everything to Bobby Brewster's hand, except turn it inside out. He tapped it and wiggled the fingers, and looked

at it through a magnifying glass. Then he leaned
back in his chair.

'In all my years of doctoring,' he said, 'I've
never met a case like this before. Bobby Brewster's hand has got banana poisoning.'

'Banana poisoning?' cried Mrs Brewster. 'What
ever is that?'

'There's no need to be alarmed,' said the doctor.
'It's not in the least dangerous. I'll give you some
ointment to rub on his hand, and I'd advise you to
keep him away from bananas in future.'

And she has.

Not that it has been a very difficult thing to do.

Bobby seems to have lost all enthusiasm for bananas since then – and so has Micky the monkey puppet. And one good result has come out of this extraordinary affair. From that day to this Bobby's antics with his glove puppet have been more lifelike than ever. All his friends love to see him playing with it, and they say that the monkey's voice he uses when he's talking is one of the funniest things they've ever heard.

After all, how can they possibly be expected to know that it's really Mickey the monkey puppet himself doing the talking? Only Bobby Brewster, you and I know that.

Roundabout horse

It was the first day of the fair, so of course Bobby
Brewster woke early. If you had been there, you
would have done the same. Indeed, perhaps there
has been a fair in your home town and you have
been awake early, full of excitement. I know I
have. Several times.

Bobby Brewster was staying with his Aunt
Beatrice and Uncle Benjamin near a small town
in the Midlands. The fair there is always particu-
larly thrilling. It stretches right down the middle
of the main street and lasts from the first Thursday
in August to the Saturday. It has been held at the
same time and in the same place for hundreds of
years.

Bobby, together with other boys and girls, had watched the caravans arrive and the lorries unloaded. He knew there were coconut shies, and boards for throwing pennies on squares. Hoop-las and swing-boats were also there, and a slide where you sit on a mat at the top and whizz round and round down to the bottom. As a matter of fact he had already decided to do without a mat, because he had been busy polishing the seat of his trousers by rubbing it hard on a grass slope.

But, best of all, Bobby Brewster knew that right in the middle of the fair was a roundabout. He had even chosen the actual animal on which he would ride. It was a horse. Of course, there were plenty of other things to choose from – a car, for instance, or a sort of aeroplane thing, or an ostrich. But, after all, anyone can ride in a car, and what's the use of an aeroplane thing that doesn't go up in the air, and who ever heard of a boy riding an ostrich? No – the horse was his definite choice. One special white horse, with large black and red spots all over it, and a snorting nose that looked as if it ought to be breathing fire, but wasn't.

Unfortunately there was an awful long time to wait before the fair opened at six o'clock. Thursday morning and afternoon during fair week are always dull, because nothing special happens. Saturday is altogether different. That afternoon there is the annual horse show and race, and everyone goes there before flocking to the fair for a grand Saturday night outing.

Bobby had been saving for the fair for a long time and had forty-five pence to spend. That may sound a lot, but it isn't all that much for a fair that lasts for three nights.

After all, a roundabout costs five pence a time, and you have to go on it at least twice to feel giddy enough to be worth the money. So on Thursday night Bobby saved the roundabout till last, just like the marzipan on a cake.

When the time came, he waited and watched the previous round, and then pounced on his special horse before any other boy could get to it. I wonder what he would have said if a small girl had asked politely, 'Please may I ride the horse and you ride the ostrich?' He usually has quite good manners, but I doubt if he would have said,

'Yes, certainly'. He would probably have found a very good reason for explaining that girls can ride much better on ostriches than horses. Anyway, luckily the question didn't arise.

The music blared and off they went. Round and round and up and down. Great fun it was. Then in the middle of a ride a very funny thing happened. The roundabout horse turned its head and spoke. It did, really.

'Are you enjoying the ride?' it asked.

'I beg your pardon?' said Bobby Brewster.

'I said are you enjoying the ride,' repeated the roundabout horse.

'It's jolly good,' said Bobby. 'But please don't turn round and talk to me like that. Everybody will stare.'

'Oh no, they won't,' said the roundabout horse.

'Why not?' asked Bobby.

'Because no one else can see or hear what I'm doing if I don't want them to,' explained the horse. 'You seem to forget that you're Bobby Brewster, the ordinary boy who has the most extraordinary adventures.'

'So I am,' said Bobby. 'I hadn't thought of that.'

Well, for the rest of the ride they went on talking, and Bobby found that, although the horse had enjoyed being on a roundabout at first, it was getting rather fed up with it.

'How would you like to spend every evening running round and round chasing an ostrich?' asked the horse.

'I should probably get tired of it after a time,' agreed Bobby.

'I've no doubt you would,' said the horse. 'Especially an ostrich with a silly expression on its face like that one. I sometimes simply long to lean forward and bite its tail feathers.'

'Then why don't you?' asked Bobby.

'I probably will some day,' said the roundabout horse.

By that time the first ride was coming to an end, and the horse said that it was very glad that Bobby was staying on for a second go, because it wanted to ask him a favour.

'What is it you want?' asked Bobby when the second ride had started.

'Just for a change, will you please enter me for the horse show and big race on Saturday afternoon?' asked the roundabout horse. 'I promise to be very quiet in spite of my snorting nostrils, and I shall probably win lots and lots of prizes for you.'

'How will you get off the roundabout?' asked Bobby.

'Leave that to me,' said the horse. 'Just be at the entrance to the show at two o'clock on Saturday afternoon, and I'll be waiting for you to lead me in. But don't tell anyone about it, or I won't come.'

As you can imagine, Bobby Brewster was very excited for the rest of the week. He even went to bed early on Friday night instead of going to the fair, so that Saturday morning would come all the sooner. Luckily it turned out to be a beautiful day. To the great surprise of Aunt Beatrice, Bobby tidied his clothes and brushed his hair without being asked before leaving for the horse show after dinner.

Sure enough, there was the white horse, with big black and red spots, waiting for him at the entrance. This time he didn't mind people staring, because he was so excited at entering a horse at the show for the first time in his life.

The difficulty was to decide what class to enter. After all, who ever heard of a white cart-horse with black and red spots? Or a pony and trap, or a riding pony either, for that matter. White, yes, and sometimes perhaps with just black spots, but white with big black and red spots – never. Luckily Bobby had saved enough money by not going to the fair on Friday night, so he decided to enter the roundabout horse for all three classes just to be on the safe side.

The judge for the events was Colonel Danvers, an important-looking man with a red face and a large moustache. He seemed as surprised as anybody to see a white cart-horse with black and red spots.

But there were much larger and stronger-looking cart-horses anyway, so he didn't give Bobby a prize for that event.

Then the decorated ponies and traps trotted into the ring. Once again the white horse with the big black and red spots was there, but it wasn't pulling a trap, so it could hardly win a prize in that class either, could it?

The last competition was for the smartest riding pony. Bobby had never ridden a real pony before, but he found no difficulty. The roundabout horse was quiet, as it had promised to be. All the people clapped loudly as he trotted it round the ring, and it really did seem at last as though he might win a prize. But it was not to be. Colonel Danvers patted the flanks of all the ponies, one after the

other, to see how silky they felt. When he patted the roundabout horse there was a loud slapping noise.

'Goodness gracious me,' cried Colonel Danvers. 'It feels like wood.'

Before you could say 'Jack Robinson' he had taken a penknife out of his pocket and was scratching one of the red spots on the roundabout horse to see if he could scrape it off. Of course he could, and did.

'It is wood,' he cried. 'I'm very sorry, but a wooden horse can't win a prize for the best riding pony.'

'Why not?' asked Bobby Brewster. 'After all, I'm riding it.'

'That makes no difference,' said Colonel Danvers. 'I'm afraid I can't alter my decision.'

Bobby felt rather disappointed about that. But he cheered up when he saw horses gathering for the start of the big race. This was the most important event of the whole afternoon. He trotted over on the roundabout horse to join them, feeling very confident.

I suppose you feel just as confident as Bobby Brewster did, don't you, and think that he won the big race easily? Well, you're wrong. When the Colonel shouted GO! all the roundabout horse could do was to run round and round in a circle and get in the way of all the other horses. I suppose that wasn't so surprising when you think of all the circles it had run every night on the roundabout. It was an awful nuisance, all the same. Some of the riders fell off and their horses bolted, and others stopped altogether to keep out of the way of the roundabout horse. Colonel Danvers got very annoyed and went even redder in the face. I'm afraid he shouted at Bobby to take his horse away. Then he disqualified them both, and started the race a second time without them.

Poor Bobby rode sadly back to the show entrance. 'You can leave me here,' said the roundabout horse. 'And don't be too disappointed. I'm sorry I didn't win all the prizes as I said. It's clear to me that *I'm* more use on a roundabout than anywhere else. After all, I'm supposed to be a roundabout horse, aren't I?'

'Never mind,' said Bobby. By this time he felt more cheerful, because he remembered about going to the fair that evening. 'I still have twenty pence, and tonight I'm jolly well going to spend five pence on the hoop-la and then ride on you three times running.'

That is exactly what he did. And during the third and last ride, a very funny thing happened.

There was a loud squawk, and the little girl riding the ostrich jumped up in the air and nearly fell off. Can you guess why? Yes, you're right. That naughty roundabout horse simply couldn't resist the temptation any longer. When no one – not even Bobby Brewster – was looking, it leant forward and gave the tail feathers of the ostrich a sharp bite.

Between you and me, I don't altogether blame it, do you?

Unfair to sardines

In the town where Bobby Brewster lives a new
supermarket has just opened. It is a very smart
affair with shining white walls and chromium all
over the place, but somehow Bobby doesn't like
going there as much as he does to Dobson's, the
family grocers. Mr Dobson looks like a grocer,
and his shop smells of coffee and cooked ham,
but the supermarket looks more like a hospital
and hardly smells at all.

However, once you've got things sorted out,
it is sometimes quite convenient. I say 'Sometimes' purposely, because when it is crowded,
it isn't convenient at all. For one thing, your legs

keep being banged by those wire baskets that everybody has to carry about, which is jolly painful. And for another, although you fill your basket quickly enough, you have to wait in a long queue to pay, which is jolly annoying. But never mind about that now.

When Mrs Brewster is busy she sometimes asks Bobby to go to the supermarket and do some shopping for her. Not for important things like meat, of course. That's far too difficult. Bobby might be asked to buy 'Best end of neck' and bring home a 'Worst end of neck' by mistake. Actually he feels very sorry for the lambs having a worst end to their necks, because it must be very awkward when they want to run and jump about. It doesn't seem to worry them, though, does it? And, anyway, never mind about that either, because it has nothing to do with the story.

One Saturday morning last year Bobby was sent to the supermarket to buy a pound of butter, a packet of cornflakes, a tin of peaches, a tin of baked beans, and a pound of pork sausages. He felt quite important, because it was a longer list than usual, and he took great care to go to the right shelves in turn. But right from the start the same funny thing kept happening. When he put his hand inside the refrigerator to take out the butter he wasn't looking, and he picked up a tin of sardines by mistake. He thought that was rather a peculiar thing to be kept in a refrigerator, but he put it back and then went for the packet of cornflakes. They were on a high shelf and he had to reach for them, but the first thing he took from the shelf was a tin of sardines again.

'I wish they kept their sardines all together in one place,' said Bobby to himself. 'Now for the

peaches.' Well, he found the peaches all right, but only after picking up another tin first. And what do you think was in it?

S—d—n—s.

And that wasn't all. There was another tin of sardines amongst the baked beans, and then, goodness me, if the first thing Bobby took out of the sausage refrigerator wasn't a tin of sardines as well. This really was too much.

'Bother the sardines,' said Bobby Brewster. And he must have said it quite loudly too, because the manager of the supermarket, who was standing just behind him, asked, 'What's wrong with the sardines, sir?'

'There's nothing wrong with them,' said Bobby Brewster. 'They're just all over the place, that's all. Wherever I go I pick up a tin of sardines. Why aren't they all kept together?'

'They are,' said the manager.

'Well, if you look at your butter, your corn-flakes, your peaches, your baked beans and your pork sausages, you'll find a tin of sardines with all of them,' said Bobby Brewster.

'Indeed, you do surprise me,' said the manager,

with a surprised look on his face. 'I'll go and tidy them up myself. Thank you for telling me.'

Bobby went to join the queue to pay, and it was quite a long one, so by the time he reached the cash register and the girl was adding up his bill, the manager returned.

'I can't understand your complaint, sir,' said the manager. 'I looked in all the places you mentioned and there wasn't a tin of sardines to be seen.'

'How extraordinary,' said Bobby – and at that moment his eyes nearly popped out of his head. Do you know why? Because something very extraordinary had happened. The girl at the cash desk was taking the last thing out of Bobby's basket to put on the bill. And what do you think it was?

A tin of sardines.

'I don't want that,' cried Bobby Brewster. 'And I'm sure I never put it in the basket.'

'Never mind, sir, I'll take it back,' said the manager in a soothing voice. He had a look on his face that clearly showed he thought that Bobby must have sardines on the brain. He wasn't rude enough to say so, but Bobby felt an awful fool all the same.

When Bobby reached home his mother was very pleased with him for being so helpful. She unpacked his basket and then made a remark that surprised him.

'You have done the shopping perfectly,' she said. 'There's just one thing too many, but it doesn't matter because we can use it later.'

'What is it?' asked Bobby.

There's really no need for me to write down her answer, is there? But I will all the same, just in case you haven't guessed.

'A tin of sardines, dear,' said Mrs Brewster.

This time, for once, Bobby was lost for words. So he picked up the tin before his mother could put it in the larder and carried it up to his bedroom. He sat in a chair, looking at it with a puzzled expression.

'It looks ordinary enough,' he said to himself.

At least he thought he said it to himself, but he can't have done, because a very funny thing happened. A voice answered him. It did, really. It said:

'Looks aren't everything.'

'I beg your pardon?' asked Bobby Brewster.

'I said looks aren't everything,' said the voice. 'I may look ordinary enough, but I'm not. I'm magic.'

'You must be,' said Bobby, 'if you're a tin of sardines that can talk.'

'That's not all I can do,' said the tin of sardines. 'You remember you kept on seeing a tin of sardines wherever you went in the supermarket?'

'Yes,' said Bobby. 'The place was full of them.'

'No it wasn't,' said the tin of sardines. 'It was me all the time. That's why the manager couldn't find any others when he looked.'

'How on earth did you jump from place to place?' asked Bobby Brewster.

'Aha – that would be giving away my magic,' said the tin of sardines. 'And I've no intention of doing that.'

'Well, what was the object of it all, anyway?' asked Bobby Brewster.

'I wanted you to bring me home,' said the tin of sardines. 'Because I needed your help and someone had told me you were very fond of sardines.'

'I am indeed,' agreed Bobby Brewster. 'And how can I help?'

'I want to protest about my packing,' said the tin of sardines. 'It's far too tight. It's unfair to sardines.'

'I always thought that was the right way to pack sardines,' said Bobby. 'After all, when lots of people are crammed into a tube train, they say they're packed like sardines.'

'That doesn't mean they're enjoying it,' said the tin of sardines. 'They're very relieved when the doors open and some people get out, I can tell you.'

'Anyway,' said Bobby, 'there's even a game called "Sardines". People all pack as closely as they can together in a small space. It's great fun.'

'A game's one thing and real life's another,' said the tin of sardines. 'You enjoy playing at soldiers, but if anyone really started shooting at you, you'd run a mile.'

'That's true,' agreed Bobby. 'Well – what do you want me to do about it?'

'I want you to write to someone in authority and protest at the condition in which sardines are packed,' said the tin of sardines.

'Very well,' said Bobby. 'Who shall I write to?'

They thought of all sorts of people. The Prime Minister probably couldn't be bothered with all the other problems on his mind, and the Minister of Food would only think of tins of sardines as food for people and not homes for sardines. Then Bobby Brewster had an idea.

'You come from Portugal,' he said, 'so I'll write to the King of Portugal.'

'Portugal hasn't got a King,' said the tin of sardines. 'It's a republic with a president.'

'Then I'll write to the President of Portugal,' said Bobby.

So that is what he did, and this is what he wrote:

Dear President of Portugal,

I have just bought a tin of sardines made in Portugal, and it is packed so tightly that it seems unfair to the sardines. Do you think it could be

*arranged for the tins to contain more oil and fewer
sardines, because then they would be far more
comfortable?*

Yours sincerely,
Bobby Brewster

Bobby had to spend five pence from his own
pocket-money to send this letter, and it must
have taken quite a time to reach the right person,
because he didn't get a reply for three weeks.
When it did arrive, however, it looked most
important and was typed in perfect English. This
is what it said:

Dear Bobby Brewster,
*In reply to your letter, I have personally
consulted many sardine experts in this country
and can assure you that if there was more oil and
fewer sardines in the tins, the sardines would bang
against each other and bruise–which would be very
painful for them and most disappointing to you,
because bruised sardines taste horrid.*
*I can assure you that in Portugal we would
never dream of being unfair to sardines.*

I have the honour to remain,
Your obedient servant,
Fernandez Lopez

When Bobby read this letter to the tin of sardines – which he had managed to hide in his bedroom desk without his mother noticing it – it thought for a moment and then said:

'I hadn't thought of that, and it was very kind of Fernandez Lopez to take so much trouble. Maybe I'm wrong, and perhaps the sardines are better off the way they are. After all, they must be very cosy. Ah well, you'd better put me back in the larder and arrange for your mother to open me up for tea. I can guarantee you'll enjoy your tea.'

So they did. And Bobby really did thoroughly enjoy his tea. Which is hardly surprising, is it, because if there is one thing he likes better than any other it's

S-rd—e s-n-w-ch-s.

Six pints, please!

Mrs Brewster can't always be in the kitchen when the milkman calls. Nor is it always possible for her to answer the back door bell when he rings it, and, anyway, sometimes she's out. So for her last birthday Bobby Brewster had a jolly good idea. He bought her one of those wooden board things for ordering milk. Do you know what I mean? A board made to look something like a clock with a hand that you can move round, only instead of telling the time it tells the milkman how many pints to leave.

Something like this:

I said it was a jolly good idea, and it was for a time. Mrs Brewster used to push the hand round to two or three pints – which is what they usually need – and then bother no more about it. But unfortunately Bobby couldn't resist fiddling with it. I think I've told you before that Bobby is inclined to fiddle with things, haven't I? Well, whenever he went out of the back door he twiddled the hand round and round. In the end it became so loose that the milkman started delivering six pints of milk whenever he called.

'I can't think what's the matter with the man,' said Mrs Brewster. 'Does he imagine that I invite all the neighbours to tea every day?' But when she asked him about it, he explained that she was *ordering* six pints of milk every day, and it was then she found that although she set the hand to two or three every morning, by the time the milkman called it had slipped down to six. Mrs Brewster tried tightening it several times, but it wasn't any good, because, without thinking, every time he went out of the back door, Bobby twiddled the hand round and made it loose again.

In the end Mrs Brewster had to give up the

idea of using the board altogether, and when Bobby heard about it he felt rather ashamed of his fiddling. But then he had another jolly good idea, and this time he didn't wait for his mother's birthday, or even for Christmas. Out of his pocket-money he bought her a smart slate and some chalk. This was kept in the back porch for Mrs Brewster to write her order out. At first she only ordered milk on it, like this:

3 pints please

but after a time she became more adventurous and twice a week ordered things from the grocer and the greengrocer as well:

$\frac{1}{2}$ *lb pork sausages*
$\frac{1}{2}$ *lb New Zealand lamb*
1 *doz standard eggs*
$\frac{1}{2}$ *lb Princess biscuits*
2 *tins sardines* or
2 *lb Cox's orange pippins*
6 *lb potatoes*
1 *lettuce*

This worked very well indeed for some time,

but then the trouble started, and again it was with the milk. One day when Mrs Brewster went to the back door to collect it she found six pints. Luckily the milkman was only just on his way out of the front gate, so she called him back to complain.

'But, madam, you *ordered* six pints,' he said, and when she looked on the slate there it was, written out:

'That's not my writing,' said Mrs Brewster.

'It isn't mine either, madam,' said the milk-man.

'Well, it seems rather extraordinary,' said Mrs Brewster, 'but I only want three pints anyway,' so she handed the other three back to the milk-man and he took them away.

The next day was grocery day, and as she had to go out, Mrs Brewster was very careful to write her order on the slate. When she got home during the afternoon this is what she found in the back porch, and, what's more, this is what was written on the slate:

6 lb tapioca
6 lb broken biscuits
6 lb Gorgonzola cheese
6 pots wild duck paste
24 tins sardines

She was gazing in amazement at this when Bobby Brewster came home from school.

'Did you come home during the lunch hour,

Bobby?' asked his mother, looking at him hard.

'No, mother,' said Bobby Brewster.

'Are you *sure* you didn't order twenty-four tins of sardines on that slate?' she asked.

'Positive,' said Bobby, and then he looked at the writing and started to laugh.

'There's nothing to laugh about,' said his mother.

'Well, it *is* rather funny, you know,' said Bobby. 'I may like sardines, but I hate the taste of tapioca pudding and the smell of Gorgonzola cheese, and I think it's awfully cruel to turn wild ducks into paste.'

'So do I,' said Mrs Brewster. 'Anyway, I mean to watch the back door carefully for somebody who writes like this, and in the meantime this lot can go back to the grocer's.'

The next day was Saturday, when the green-grocer calls with his mobile shop. Mrs Brewster wrote her order on the slate and listened carefully for footsteps at the back door. But there weren't any until about eleven o'clock, when the bell rang, and when she opened it, there was the greengrocer himself.

'Good morning, madam,' he said. 'Excuse my ringing the bell, but do you *really* want this order?' And he pointed to the slate.

Written on it, quite plain to see, were the words:

    12 lb mouldy potatoes
     6 boxes sticky dates
     6 boxes squashy bananas
     6 lb rotten tomatoes

'Certainly not,' cried Mrs Brewster. 'Who ever heard of such a thing?'

'I *thought* it might be a mistake, madam,' said the greengrocer.

'That's not *my* writing,' said Mrs Brewster.

'It's not mine either, madam,' said the greengrocer.

'Nor mine,' said Bobby Brewster, who had been in the kitchen when his mother answered the bell.

'I *do* want these things,' said Mrs Brewster. 'But not the sort written on the slate. Please deliver me six pounds of King Edward potatoes, *not* mouldy, one box of dates, *not* too sticky, one bunch of bananas, *not* over-ripe, and one pound of tomatoes, *not* rotten.'

'Certainly, madam,' said the greengrocer, and he collected the order from his van.

When he had left and Mrs Brewster had gone indoors, Bobby was still standing in the porch gazing at the writing on the slate.

'I wonder whose writing that is?' he said to himself.

At least, he thought he said it to himself, but he can't have done, because a voice answered him. It did, really. It said:

'Mine.'

'I beg your pardon?' asked Bobby Brewster.

'I said it's *my* writing,' said the voice. 'I wrote it on myself.'

'Who are you?' asked Bobby Brewster.

'I'm your mother's slate,' said the voice. 'And I'm magic.'

'You jolly well must be,' said Bobby Brewster. 'I may have written silly things on my own forehead when I've got nothing better to do, but then *I've* got hands to write with. I don't see *how* a slate can write words on itself, however magic it is.'

'I didn't exactly *write* the words,' said the slate. 'I just used my magic to make them appear.'

'Why?' asked Bobby Brewster.

'Just for fun,' said the slate. 'I was so tired of ordering the same old things time after time, that I thought I would have a little joke.'

'Well, my mother didn't think it was very

funny,' said Bobby, 'and suppose the green-grocer hadn't rung the bell and had really delivered the mouldy potatoes, sticky dates, squashy bananas, and rotten tomatoes?'

'That would have been funnier still,' said the slate.

'Yes, perhaps it would,' said Bobby Brewster, and he started to laugh.

'Anyway, now I've *had* my joke and you *know* I'm magic, I want you to give me the chance of being even magicer,' said the slate.

'How?' asked Bobby.

'Will you please tell your mother not to bother to write orders on me any more?' said the slate. 'I know exactly what you want, and I'll arrange the ordering myself.'

'I'll try,' said Bobby, 'but I don't know what she'll say.' He thought his mother would think the whole idea rather peculiar.

And she did.

'Who ever heard of such a thing?' she asked. 'Besides, we might find ourselves eating nothing but broken biscuits, wild duck paste, and rotten tomatoes.'

'I'm *sure* we won't, Mother,' said Bobby. 'The magic slate only ordered the things for fun, so that we would find out how magic it was. *Do* try it. After all, if it *does* work it'll save you a lot of trouble.'

So she did. And it *did* work. And it saved her *lots and lots* of trouble. Before the magic slate took over the ordering, Mrs Brewster was always saying: 'Oh dear, *what* shall I order for supper?' or 'What on *earth* shall we have for lunch tomorrow?' Now she never needs to worry, because the slate orders everything for her. Very carefully, too. They never have the same food two days running, and it never orders anything too expensive. Nor does it allow the tradesmen to leave any inferior goods. Oh dear me, no. When there could be any doubts, it gives clear instructions, such as:

One cabbage — with plenty of heart

  or

Two grapefruit — nice juicy ones

What is more, when ordering from the grocer

it knows when there are any special offers, and
never misses an opportunity to say:

One tin of coffee — reduced from 18p
to 15p

    or

One packet of cornflakes — with free balloon

But even that's not all. Since then the Brewsters have found that the slate is even more magic
than they realized. Whenever they want people
to know where they are, all they have to do is

to go out by the back door and say something like:

'*I'm going for a walk.*'

or

'*We're going shopping.*'

or

'*I'm going to the hairdresser's.*'

Then when people call they read on the slate:

'*She's gone for a walk.*'

or

'*They're out shopping.*'

or

'*He's having a haircut.*'

But the most amazing thing happens every Sunday morning. The Brewsters always leave the house by the *front* door, but the slate must know what day of the week it is and where they go, because when the milkman calls at the back door later in the morning, he always reads the same message:

Three pints please, one small carton cream.
Gone to church.